Dear Parents and Educators,

Welcome to Penguin Young Readers! As parents and educators, you know that each child develops at his or her own pace—in terms of speech, critical thinking, and, of course, reading. Penguin Young Readers recognizes this fact. As a result, each Penguin Young Readers book is assigned a traditional easy-to-read level (1–4) as well as a Guided Reading Level (A–P). Both of these systems will help you choose the right book for your child. Please refer to the back of each book for specific leveling information. Penguin Young Readers features esteemed authors and illustrators, stories about favorite characters, fascinating nonfiction, and more!

Madeline and Her Dog

LEVEL **2**

GUIDED READING LEVEL **H**

This book is perfect for a **Progressing Reader** who:
- can figure out unknown words by using picture and context clues;
- can recognize beginning, middle, and ending sounds;
- can make and confirm predictions about what will happen in the text; and
- can distinguish between fiction and nonfiction.

Here are some **activities** you can do during and after reading this book:
- Rhyming Words: On a separate sheet of paper, make a list of all the rhyming words in this story. For example, *place* rhymes with *face*, so write those two words next to each other. Some words may have more than one rhyming word (hint: line).
- Comprehension: Answer the following questions about the story.
  - Why do the people on the street think Genevieve is stinky?
  - After Genevieve's bath, why does Miss Clavel say, "For heaven's sake!"?
  - Why does Genevieve end up in the tub again at the end of the story?

Remember, sharing the love of reading with a child is the best gift you can give!

—Bonnie Bader, EdM
 Penguin Young Readers program

*Penguin Young Readers are leveled by independent reviewers applying the standards developed by Irene Fountas and Gay Su Pinnell in *Matching Books to Readers: Using Leveled Books in Guided Reading*, Heinemann, 1999.

Penguin Young Readers
Published by the Penguin Group
Penguin Group (USA) Inc., 375 Hudson Street, New York, New York 10014, USA
Penguin Group (Canada), 90 Eglinton Avenue East, Suite 700, Toronto, Ontario M4P 2Y3, Canada
(a division of Pearson Penguin Canada Inc.)
Penguin Books Ltd., 80 Strand, London WC2R 0RL, England
Penguin Group Ireland, 25 St. Stephen's Green, Dublin 2, Ireland (a division of Penguin Books Ltd.)
Penguin Group (Australia), 250 Camberwell Road, Camberwell, Victoria 3124, Australia
(a division of Pearson Australia Group Pty. Ltd.)
Penguin Books India Pvt. Ltd., 11 Community Centre, Panchsheel Park, New Delhi—110 017, India
Penguin Group (NZ), 67 Apollo Drive, Rosedale, Auckland 0632, New Zealand
(a division of Pearson New Zealand Ltd.)
Penguin Books (South Africa) (Pty.) Ltd., 24 Sturdee Avenue,
Rosebank, Johannesburg 2196, South Africa

Penguin Books Ltd., Registered Offices: 80 Strand, London WC2R 0RL, England

Library of Congress Cataloging-in-Publication Data is available.

ISBN 978-0-448-45438-2 (pbk)   10 9 8 7 6 5 4 3 2 1
ISBN 978-0-448-45734-5 (hc)   10 9 8 7 6 5 4 3 2 1

PENGUIN YOUNG READERS

LEVEL
PROGRESSING
READER
2

MADELINE
AND HER DOG

written by John Bemelmans Marciano
illustrated by JT Morrow
based on the art of John Bemelmans Marciano

Penguin Young Readers
An Imprint of Penguin Group (USA) Inc.

In an old house in Paris

that is covered in vines,

live twelve little girls

in two straight lines.

The smallest one is Madeline.

The girls get dressed

by half past nine.

But Madeline will never leave

without her puppy, Genevieve.

Genevieve sniffs

along the streets,

on the hunt for tasty treats.

A garbage can

is the perfect place

for Genevieve to stuff her face.

Genevieve gets

her dearest wish.

From the river,

she pulls a fish!

"Pee-yew!" say the people

all around.

"That is one dirty,

stinky hound!"

Miss Clavel says,

"We must go right away

and wash this dog

without delay!"

Genevieve thinks,

"Something is not right!"

The pooch puts up a mighty fight.

But she is outnumbered—

that's basic math.

The girls lift her—

SPLASH!

—right into the bath.

They wash their pup

from tail to snout.

As hard as she tries,

she can't get out.

With a rub-a-dub-dub

comes the final

rinse and scrub.

She gives a wiggle

and a great big SHAKE.

Miss Clavel says,

"For heaven's sake!"

The girls pat her dry.

The bath is done.

Madeline says,

"Now wasn't that fun?"

Genevieve races

for the door.

The girls forgot

to close it before.

In the garden, she digs a hole.

What a perfect spot to roll!

Madeline says,

"Genevieve, no!

Come out right now!"

But the dog won't go.

At last Madeline

wins the fight.

But she and her dog

are quite a sight!

Now there is a tub for two.

All we need in the bath

is YOU!